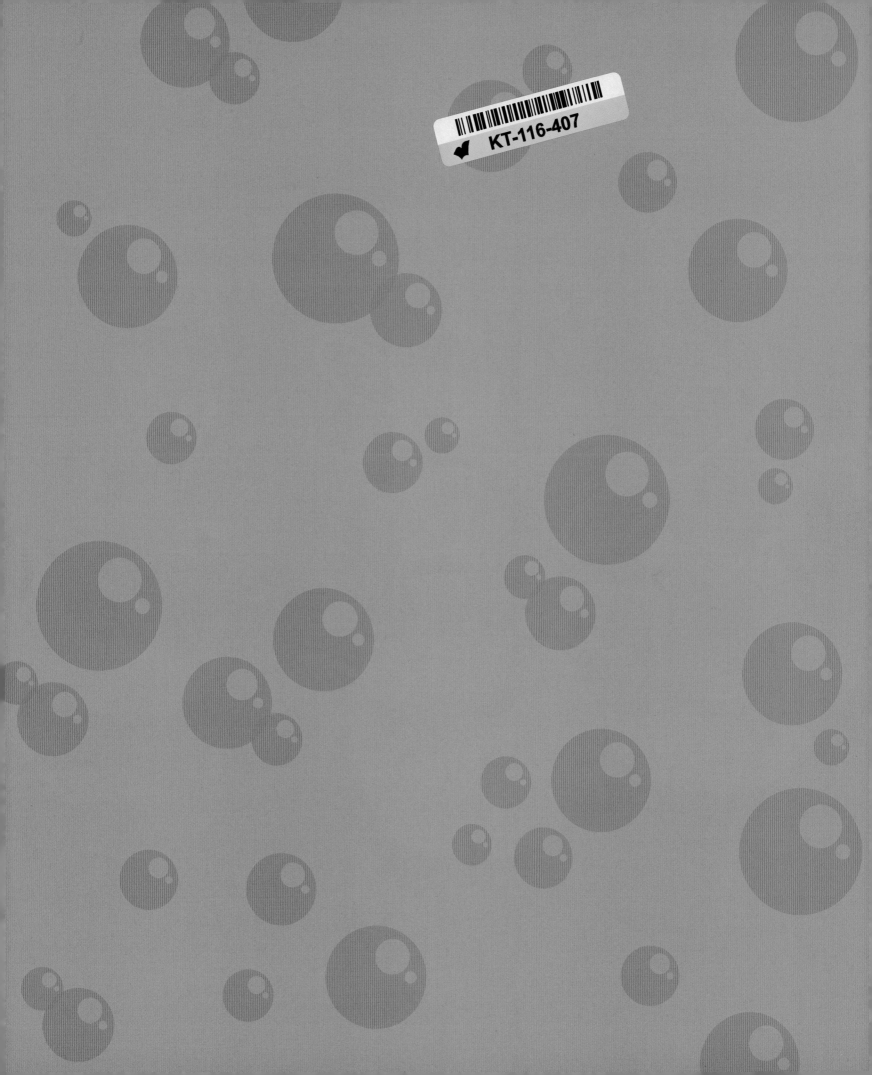

This edition published by Parragon Books Ltd in 2014
Parragon Books Ltd
Chartist House
15–17 Trim Street
Bath BA1 1HA, UK
www.parragon.com

Written by Sheila Sweeny Higginson
Based on the episode by Kent Redeker
Based on the series created by Chris Nee

ISBN 978-1-4723-4278-2

Printed in China

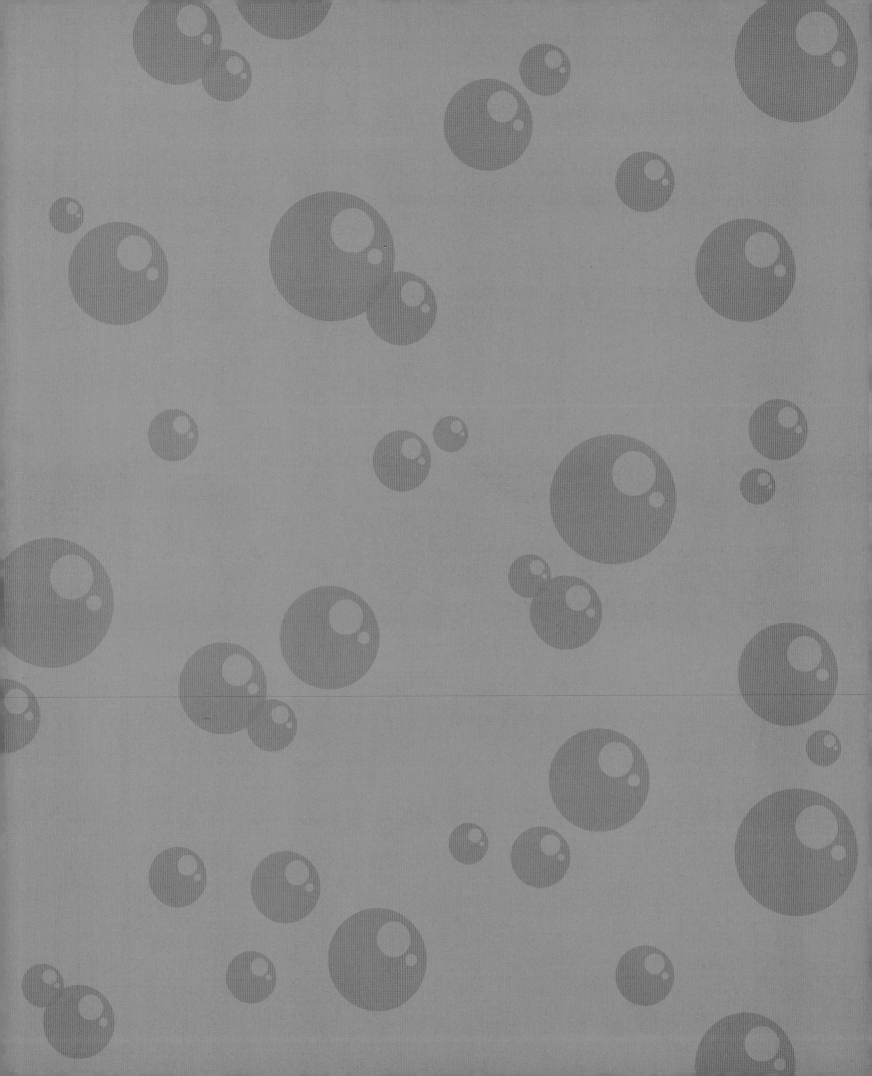

Bubble Trouble

PaRragon

Bath · New York · Cologne · Melbourne · Delhi
Hong Kong · Shenzhen · Singapore · Amsterdam

Bubbles, bubbles everywhere! Alma pops three bubbles, Emmie pops six. Doc pops two bubbles at once! Emmie's dog Rudi wants to pop bubbles, too.

But Bubble Monkey isn't working any more.

She's all out of bubbles.

Doc takes Bubble Monkey to the clinic and brings her to life with the magic stethoscope.

"Hey, look!" Stuffy says. "Doc brought Bubble Monkey over to play."

"Sorry, Stuffy, but Bubble Monkey is here for a check-up," says Doc.

Next, Doc listens to Bubble Monkey's chest.

"It sounds like gloop is blocking your bubble pumper,"
she says. "Are you having any other symptoms?"

"What are symptoms?" asks Bubble Monkey.
Doc explains that symptoms are things that hurt.

"It's your body's way of telling you that something is wrong."

"Well, I have a tummy ache," Bubble Monkey says.

"Can I give your tummy a little squeeze?" Doc asks.
She presses Bubble Monkey's stomach. Something shoots
out and hits Stuffy in the chest!

"Ick!" says Stuffy.

Now Stuffy and Chilly are stuck together!

"Weird," says Doc as she pulls them apart.

Doc looks closely at the gloop on Stuffy's chest.

"This isn't bubble soap," says Doc. "This is glue.

That's why Bubble Monkey is all blocked up!"

Doc heads back to Emmie's garden to investigate.

"Alma, what did you put in Bubble Monkey?" she asks.

Alma holds up the pink jar. "I used this," she says.

"Alma, the pink one is glue!" Emmie says. "The green one is the bubble soap!"

"Toys need to be filled up right, just like people need to eat well," explains Doc.

Then Doc cleans out Bubble Monkey's tubes
and fills her up with bubble soap.

"Thanks, Doc. I feel better!" Bubble Monkey cheers.
"You're super fantastic!"

"I love my job!" says Doc. "Now let's get you back to
Emmie and Alma."

"I'm back!" Doc says. "And, this time, I brought Bubble Monkey!"

"Did you fix her?" Alma asks.

"There's only one way to find out," says Doc.

Bubbles!

Doc's Tips on Eating Well

- We have to eat the right things to make our bodies healthy and feel good.

- Eat a good breakfast each morning.

- Cut down on sweets.

- Eat plenty of healthy fruits and vegetables.

- Try to stay away from fried, fatty foods.

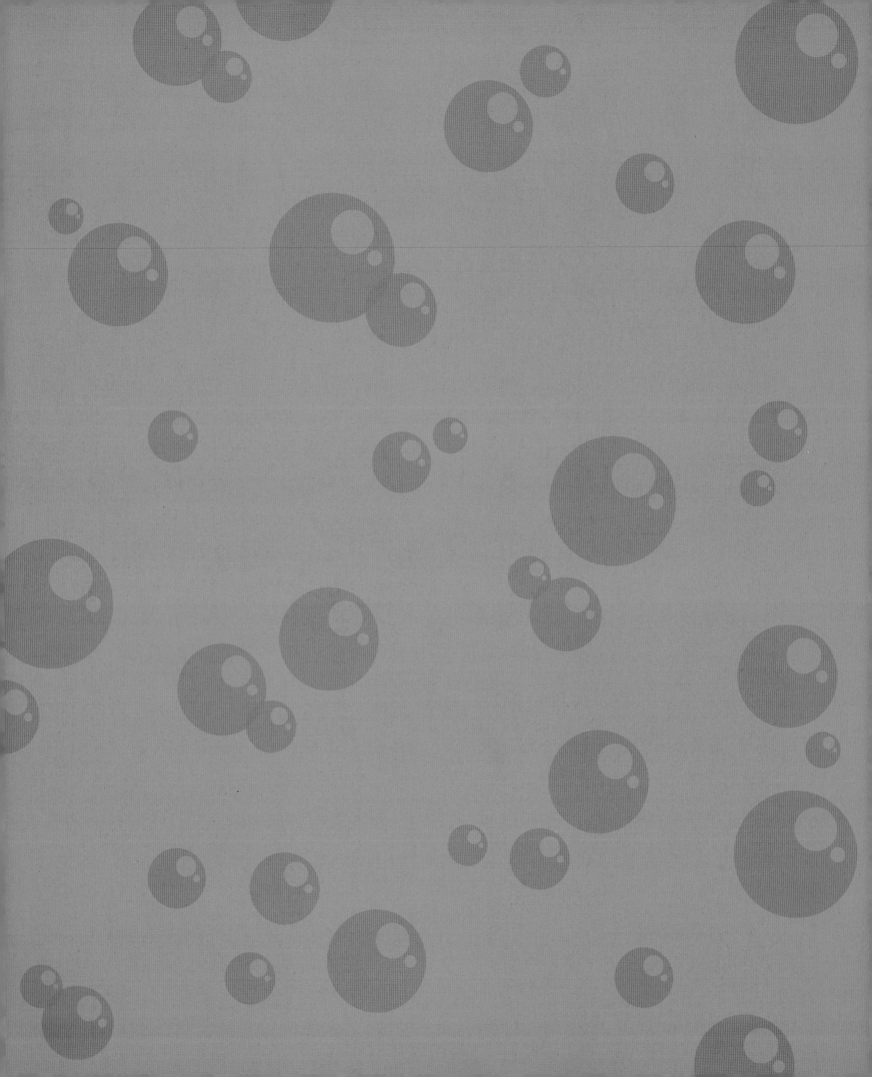

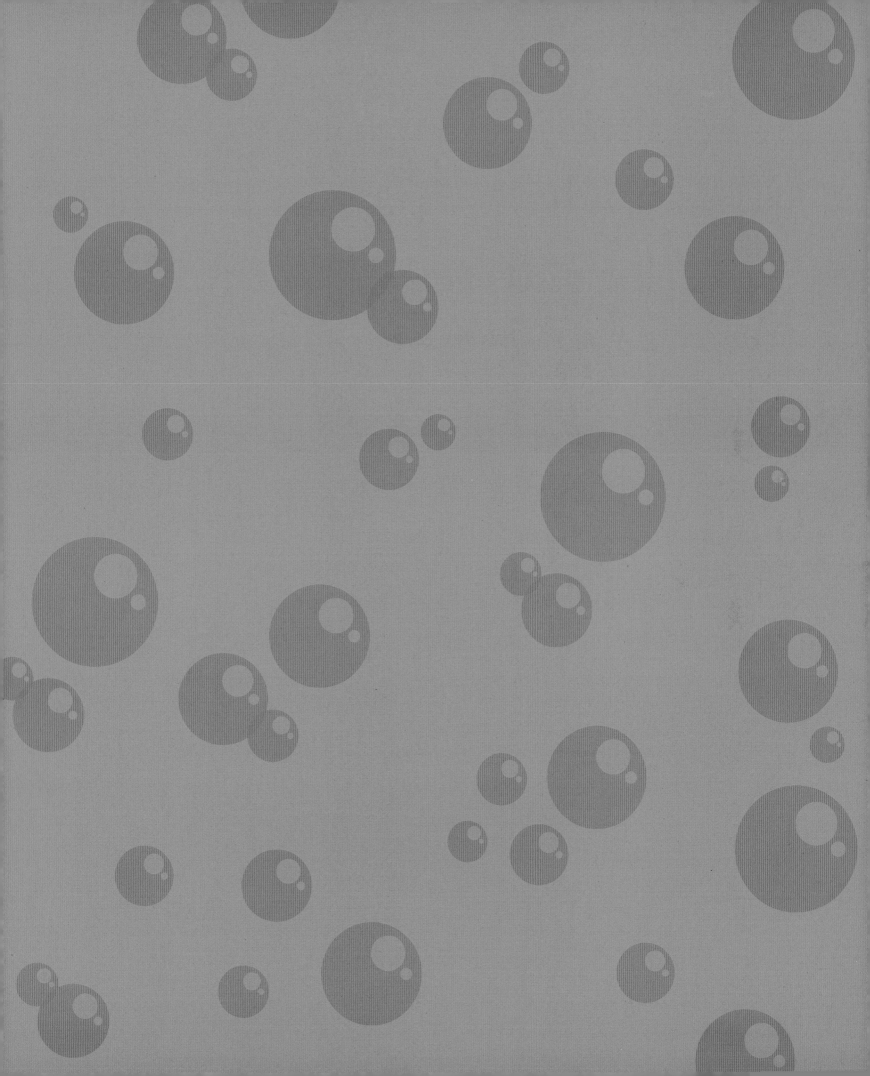